To Jessie, Lily, and Nathan
with love and thanks for the adventures we share.

— Adam

To my Henry and Emily
whom I hope to inspire to pursue big dreams!

— Andrew

www.mascotbooks.com

Lunchbox Adventures®: Dive Deep

For more information, please contact:
Mascot Books
620 Herndon Parkway, Suite 320
Herndon, VA 20170
info@mascotbooks.com

Library of Congress Control Number: 2019914870

CPSIA Code: PRTWP1219A
ISBN: 978-1-64307-379-8

Printed in Malaysia

LUNCHBOX Adventures®

DIVE DEEP

ADAM & ANDREW PEEPLES

ARTWORK BY ANDREW LAITINEN

AUTHOR'S NOTE

Dear Readers,

We are excited for you to join us in the first of many Lunchbox Adventures with Blaze and Ashley!

We hope this series inspires you to live the Adventure Makers Code:

- Pursue big dreams

- Be adventurous

- Make a difference

Visit www.lunchboxadventures.com for more stories, information, and fun activities!

Sincerely,
Adam & Andrew Peeples

TABLE OF CONTENTS

Hi!

My name is Blaze. Today was a great day! It was my birthday. And even more importantly, today I learned about Adventure Makers!

The day started with a big breakfast and a present from my dad, Fire Chief Knight. The present was a new lunchbox! Well, it is actually an old metal lunchbox, but I love it! It is special because my dad has been saving it for me since I was baby. And it's my favorite color — fire engine red!

Inside the lunchbox was a mysterious note. The note said, "When the boy turns nine, give him this lunchbox, and the adventures will begin!" No one knows who wrote the note. But the note was right!

My class went on a field trip today to the Science & History Museum. That is where I discovered that my lunchbox has magical powers! My best friend Ashley was with me when my lunchbox took us on a magical adventure. We dove deep into the sea in a submarine and found a great hidden treasure!

I can't wait to share my adventure with you! Let's go!

Blaze

THE BIRTHDAY GIFT

Blaze chomped down his last bite of chocolate cake like a hungry shark.

"Mmmmm," said Blaze. "Chocolate cake is my favorite!"

Blaze's dad, Fire Chief Knight, had packed the chocolate cake as a special treat in Blaze's lunchbox because today was his ninth birthday.

"Is that a new lunchbox?" asked Ashley. "It's really cool!"

Ashley was sitting with Blaze in the cafeteria of the Science & History Museum. Their class was on a field trip with their teacher, Miss Amy, to see three new exhibits. The class was starting with the Undersea exhibit. Then they planned to learn about the History of Flight and the International Space Station.

"It is cool! My dad gave it to me for my birthday," said Blaze. "He said the lunchbox is an antique and is very special. It's made of metal and looks old, but I love it! It's the same color as the fire trucks at my house!"

Blaze lived with Fire Chief Knight in an apartment above the firehouse.

Ashley pointed to the lunchbox. "What's that silver emblem on the side? It looks like a mountain inside of a circle."

"I'm not sure," said Blaze. "But it's the same emblem that is on this note that came with it."

Blaze excitedly opened the lunchbox and pulled out a folded piece of paper and handed it to Ashley. On the outside of the note was the same emblem of a mountain with a circle around it.

Ashley opened the note and read it aloud, "'When the boy turns nine, give him this lunchbox and the adventures will begin!' Whoa!" Then she asked, "What does it mean? Do you know who wrote it?"

"Nobody knows," said Blaze. "The note was inside the lunchbox when the firefighters found me."

Blaze was found when he was a baby by Fire Chief Knight and the firefighters of Station #53 on the steps of their firehouse. The lunchbox had been the only thing with him. When Blaze's family could not be found, Fire Chief Knight adopted him.

"My dad followed the instructions on the note and gave me the lunchbox today for my birthday," Blaze explained.

"Your dad is the best!" said Ashley.

All around them, the other students had gathered their lunchboxes and were leaving the cafeteria.

"Come on!" said Blaze excitedly. "The class is already heading inside."

"Race you!" said Ashley.

"You're on!" Blaze said. He grabbed his lunchbox and put the strap over his shoulder.

Ashley jumped from her chair and ran past Blaze toward the open doors of the Undersea exhibit. Blaze ran to catch up.

LUNCHBOX MAGIC! ②

Ashley and Blaze ran through the doors of the Undersea exhibit.

"Wow!" said Blaze. "Look at that submarine!"

"It looks like the one from our science and history book!" said Ashley.

In the middle of the Undersea exhibit was an enormous submarine. It was bright red, like Blaze's lunchbox. Miss Amy stood in front of the submarine as the class gathered around.

"Class. As you know, I volunteer here at the museum on the weekends," said Miss Amy. "I helped create this Undersea exhibit. My favorite part is this submarine. The submarine was donated to the museum after the adventurer who owned the vessel mysteriously disappeared. It's rumored she found great treasures hidden

inside a secret sunken ship!"

"Hidden treasure!" Blaze whispered to Ashley. "Can you imagine what it would feel like to find a sunken ship with treasure inside?"

Blaze excitedly raised his hand to ask a question.

"Did they ever find the adventurer who disappeared?" he asked.

"No," said Miss Amy, "it remains a mystery. No one has been able to find her or the secret ship since."

Miss Amy looked up at the giant clock on the wall of the exhibit. The clock was made from an old ship's wheel used to steer boats.

"Okay, class. It is 12:40 P.M. now," Miss Amy pointed to the large clock. "Meet back here in 20 minutes, at 1:00 P.M. And remember, this is an interactive museum. You can touch the exhibits. And you can climb inside the submarine. When you do, I hope you imagine having a real adventure in the ocean!"

Miss Amy dismissed the class to explore the exhibit. Some students began lining up to go inside the submarine. Others walked around the exhibit. There was a deep-sea diving suit on display and an aquarium full of colorful fish.

Ashley and Blaze slowly moved forward as they waited in the long line to climb into the submarine.

"Finally, it's our turn!" Ashley pointed. "The clock says 12:55. We only have five minutes left before we have to leave the exhibit!"

Ashley grabbed the ladder and quickly climbed to the top of the submarine. Then she disappeared through the open hatch.

"Wait for me!" said Blaze. "You know I don't like heights."

Blaze's hands trembled as he carefully climbed each rung of the ladder.

When he made it to the top of the submarine, Blaze swung his legs down into the open hatch and climbed inside.

"I've never seen anything like this!" said Blaze as he looked around.

The walls, ceiling, and floor were all made of a silver metal. There were pipes running along the curved walls from the front to the back of the boat. At the front there was a control panel and a large window.

"Look!" Blaze pointed. "We can see the Undersea exhibit outside. There's our class and Miss Amy!"

"Can you imagine going on an adventure to explore the real ocean?" asked Ashley.

"It would be amazing!" answered Blaze. "We could hunt

for a sunken ship with hidden treasure!"

Suddenly, Blaze's lunchbox began to vibrate. It shook so hard that the strap fell off his shoulder.

The lunchbox hit the floor of the submarine with a loud CLANK! It continued to vibrate.

"Whoa! What's happening to your lunchbox?" Ashley asked.

"I have no idea!" answered Blaze.

The silver emblem on the side of the lunchbox began to glow. The glow grew brighter and brighter and the lunchbox shook even more.

Blaze slowly reached down and touched the glowing emblem.

Immediately, the air around Blaze and Ashley began to swirl. Bright lights flashed all the colors of the rainbow. Blaze and Ashley felt weightless, like they were floating.

Then...POP! A loud sound filled their ears. Blaze and Ashley both fell to the floor.

"What was that?" asked Ashley.

"I don't know," said Blaze.

Blaze and Ashley looked around. The submarine hatch had closed and the window turned blue.

"Look!" said Ashley, as she pointed to the window. "That's not the museum!"

Blaze jumped up and ran to the window.

"The class has gone," said Blaze. "And there's water in every direction!"

TOOLS FOR SUCCESS

3

"**W**here are we?" wondered Blaze.

Water surrounded the submarine as far as Blaze and Ashley could see.

"I think we're in the ocean," answered Ashley.

Ashley looked around and then back down at Blaze's lunchbox.

"It was your lunchbox!" Ashley exclaimed. "Your lunchbox transported us here!"

"What? Like magic?" asked Blaze.

"It must be!" she said. "Your lunchbox vibrated. Then it glowed. And when you touched that sliver emblem, we came here!"

"You're right!" said Blaze. "I knew my new lunchbox was special. My dad told me so when he gave it to me. And the note that came with it said I would go on adventures!"

The lunchbox was no longer vibrating. It had sprung open on the floor.

Blaze sat down next to Ashley, and they looked inside the lunchbox to find a notebook and three small objects, each the size of a keychain charm.

"Where did those come from?" asked Ashley.

"This is weird," answered Blaze. "I've never seen these things before."

Ashley picked up the notebook. It had a hard green cover, and the corners of the book looked worn. On the front was a title that read, *Undersea Field Journal.* Below the title was the emblem of the mountain surrounded by a circle. She opened it and began scanning the pages.

"The field journal has all kinds of information about the ocean!" said Ashley.

She quickly flipped through all the pages to the very end.

"There are places for us to draw pictures and write our own observations," said Ashley. "There are already a few handwritten notes in the journal. And it looks like a page is missing from the back."

"What were the pictures at the beginning?" asked Blaze.

Ashley flipped back to the first pages of the journal.

"Those are pictures and descriptions for the other items

in the lunchbox!" said Ashley.

She pointed at the first object as she continued, "That one is a miniature deep-sea diving suit. The journal says a diving suit is needed to breathe deep underwater."

"That one is a butterfly net," said Ashley, as she pointed to the second item. "It is used to catch small fish."

Then she pointed to the third item. "And that one is a skeleton key."

"Cool! I wonder what it opens," said Blaze.

He reached into the lunchbox and slowly picked up the key.

As they both watched, the key grew larger in Blaze's hand until it was almost as large as the lunchbox itself.

"Whoa!" said Ashley. "Did you see that? The key just grew twice as big!"

"How is this happening?!" exclaimed Blaze.

"It must be the same magic that transported us here," said Ashley.

"I bet you're right," said Blaze. "I have an idea! Let's see if the key gets smaller when I put it back in the lunchbox."

Blaze slowly lowered the key back into the lunchbox. The key shrank smaller and smaller until it was miniature again.

"It is back to its original size!" said Ashley. "It *is* magic!"

Just then, Blaze and Ashley heard a loud squealing noise from outside the submarine.

"What was that?" asked Blaze.

A gray shape streaked past the submarine window, and then there was another squeal.

"There it is again!" said Blaze.

Ashley and Blaze both jumped up and stared out the window in amazement.

LEAD THE WAY

4

Staring back at Blaze and Ashley through the window was a large gray animal.

"It's a dolphin!" said Ashley excitedly.

The dolphin nodded its head up and down and squealed.

"I think she sees us!" said Blaze.

The dolphin squealed again and turned to swim away.

"She wants us to follow her!" said Blaze. He looked around then asked, "How do we make the submarine go?"

"Maybe the field journal knows!" said Ashley.

She flipped pages and began reading to herself.

"Aha!" she said. Then she moved to stand in front of the control panel.

"The levers on this panel control the propeller and steer the submarine," said Ashley. She pointed to each lever.

"Find the one that makes it go!" said Blaze. "The dolphin is swimming away."

Ashley grabbed the lever for the propeller and pushed it forward. The propeller began moving the submarine quickly through the water.

"She went that way," Blaze pointed. "Toward that coral reef. Let's catch up!"

Ashley used the other levers to steer the submarine and caught up to the dolphin right next to the coral reef. The dolphin began swimming in big circles and wiggling its flippers at Ashley and Blaze.

"What a playful dolphin!" said Ashley. "We should give her a name."

"Okay," said Blaze. "How about you pick the name?"

"Hmm, let's pick something fun," said Ashley. "How about Daphne!"

"That works for me," said Blaze. "Hi, Daphne!" he shouted.

Out by the reef, Daphne the dolphin squealed in delight.

"She loves it!" said Ashley.

The reef behind Daphne was made of coral of all different colors and shapes. Fish were swimming in and out of holes in the reef.

"Look at all the colors," said Ashley. "It's beautiful!"

"I think I see seahorses!" said Blaze. He pointed to several small sea creatures with faces like a horse.

"Hold on," said Ashley. "I think the field journal has a whole section on coral reefs!"

Ashley opened the journal and found the right page.

"It says that *boy* seahorses carry the eggs until they hatch, not girl seahorses," said Ashley.

"That's something I wouldn't have guessed," said Blaze. "What's that one?"

He pointed to a bright orange fish with white stripes. It was swimming through something that looked like bright blue hair.

"That's a clown fish!" said Ashley. "And it's hiding in an anemone. Clown fish can hide in anemone because they are immune to the sting," said Ashley. "It protects them from predator fish."

Blaze and Ashley heard another squeal.

"Look!" said Blaze. "Daphne is swimming toward a hole in the side of the reef. I think she wants us to follow."

Ashley steered the submarine closer to the hole in the reef.

"It looks like a cave!" she said.

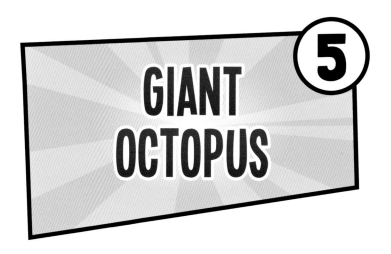

GIANT OCTOPUS

5

"**W**hat are those?" asked Blaze.

Little creatures with tentacles were swimming out of the cave.

"They look like octopuses!" said Ashley. "But they must be babies."

Daphne was swimming around the cave and squealing.

"Daphne sounds scared!" said Blaze. "I wonder what she wants us to do."

Just then, the submarine shuddered, and an enormous white and gray creature swam in front of the window. Its mouth was open and filled with rows of jagged teeth. There was a long scar across its face and down its side.

"Oh no!" shouted Ashley. "I think it's a great white shark! Look at those teeth!"

"Whoa!" shouted Blaze. "The shark is chasing the octopus babies!"

"We have to help!" said Ashley.

All of a sudden, the water surrounding the submarine swirled and turned black. The room went dark. It was as if the lights were switched off.

"What just happened?" asked Blaze.

The dark cloud in front of the window began to clear. As the cloud went away, a shape took form.

"It's a giant octopus!" exclaimed Ashley. "See her eight tentacles?"

"Yes! And her skin is bright orange," said Blaze. "Did the octopus turn the water black?"

"Of course!" said Ashley. "The field journal says an octopus will shoot ink to confuse predators and escape from danger."

"Look!" pointed Blaze. "The shark is swimming away!"

"That must be the mom octopus," said Ashley. "She was protecting her babies from the shark!"

"We should name her too!" said Blaze. "What do you think about calling her Ollie?"

The large octopus spun her arms, changing color from orange to green and back to orange.

"Did you see that?" said Ashley. "Ollie must be showing us that she loves her name! An octopus can also change colors to camouflage itself."

Ollie and Daphne swam in circles around the mouth of the cave.

"The cave must be where Ollie and her babies live," said Blaze.

"That's why Daphne brought us here!" exclaimed Ashley. "Ollie needs help getting her babies to safety."

"What if the shark comes back?" asked Blaze.

"The octopus babies will be in danger again," said Ashley. "We have to hurry! But what can we do?"

Ashley and Blaze looked helplessly at one another.

A MAGIC SUIT

"I have an idea!" said Blaze excitedly. "Maybe I can use the diving suit to go out in the water to help."

Blaze opened the lunchbox and grabbed the miniature diving suit. Slowly, he began lifting the diving suit out of the lunchbox.

"It's growing just like the key did!" Ashley exclaimed.

The diving suit grew larger and larger. Then, suddenly, it began to roll itself over Blaze's arm and across his chest.

"The suit is wrapping itself around me!" exclaimed Blaze.

Ashley watched in stunned silence as the diving suit molded itself over Blaze's body. When the suit finally settled into place, it covered Blaze from his fingertips to his toes. Only Blaze's head was left uncovered. The suit's helmet was clipped to his back by hooks attached to the suit.

"It fits perfectly!" said Blaze as he twisted his body in the suit.

"Let me help you with the helmet," said Ashley.

Ashley unhooked the helmet and gently put it on Blaze's head. Then she snapped it into place with the clips on the neck of the suit.

"The helmet has to be put on just right," said Ashley. "Otherwise, water would get in and you wouldn't be able to breathe."

Daphne squealed again.

"Did you hear that?" asked Ashley. "The dolphin sounds agitated. We have to hurry!"

Blaze grabbed the ladder and began to climb up to the hatch.

"No, wait!" said Ashley. "Don't open the hatch! The air will get out and water will fill the submarine."

"Then how should I get out of here?" asked Blaze.

Ashley flipped through the field journal.

"The field journal says that submarines have a diving hatch in the bottom," said Ashley. "The pressure of the water will keep the air trapped inside the submarine."

Blaze found the diving door and turned the wheel to open it.

"Wait!" said Ashley. "Take the butterfly net with you.

You can use it to catch the octopus babies."

Ashley reached into the lunchbox and gently pulled out the miniature butterfly net. It grew and grew until it was longer than her arms. She handed the net to Blaze.

"Good luck!" said Ashley.

"Thanks!" said Blaze. Then he carefully climbed down into the water.

ROUND UP

7

Blaze floated in front of the submarine. He realized he was still holding his breath and slowly exhaled. Then with great courage, Blaze took his first breath underwater in the suit.

"I'm breathing underwater!" said Blaze. "This diving suit is amazing!"

Ashley could hear him through the intercom on the control panel but was distracted by the field journal.

"Oh no!" Ashley exclaimed. "The field journal says sharks don't normally attack humans. But there is a handwritten note that says 'Beware of the great white shark with the scar.' The shark we just saw had a long scar down its side!"

Daphne swam in front of the cave and squealed.

"We can't worry about that now," said Blaze. "We have to help Ollie get her octopus babies to safety."

Blaze kicked the flippers on his feet and shot forward through the water to the cave opening.

"Ashley, the cave is full of octopus babies!" said Blaze.

"We were right!" said Ashley. "That must be where the octopuses live so that they are safe from the shark."

Daphne squealed and nodded her head, and Ollie spun her tentacles in agreement.

"Okay," said Blaze. "Help me spot the babies."

Over the next several minutes, Ashley, Daphne, and Ollie pointed out octopus babies all around the reef. Blaze used the butterfly net to gently scoop them up.

"I think I have the last one!" called Blaze.

"That makes ten octopus babies," said Ashley. "Nice job!"

Daphne squealed and Ollie swam a happy circle around Blaze.

"I'm going to put them back into the cave where they belong," said Blaze.

He gently shook the net inside the cave. The octopus babies swam free and joined the other babies already inside.

"Your babies are safe!" Blaze said to Ollie.

Ollie spun in a circle of delight, and her body changed color from orange to green to purple and back to orange.

"Did you see Ollie change colors?" asked Ashley. "The

field journal says an octopus can change color, but I didn't expect it to happen so fast."

Ollie stopped spinning, lifted one long arm, and gently handed Blaze a small object.

"What is it?" asked Ashley.

"I'm not sure," said Blaze. "It looks like a little pink rock filled with holes."

"It must be a piece of coral!" said Ashley. "Ollie is thanking you for helping her find her babies."

"Thank you, Ollie!" said Blaze.

Ollie spun in a circle and shifted colors to match the colors of the reef. Then she moved to the mouth of the cave.

"Look! Ollie changed colors to blend in with the reef, and now she is going to squish into the cave," said Ashley. "The field journal says octopuses don't have bones, so they can squeeze into tight spaces."

Ollie scrunched smaller and smaller and pushed her way into the cave.

"Maybe octopuses have some magic too!" said Blaze. "Ollie squeezed into the cave just like the diving suit and butterfly net fit into the lunchbox!"

Daphne squealed again. This time the sound was louder and more frantic.

"Look out, Blaze!" shouted Ashley. "The shark is coming back!"

WILD RIDE

8

Blaze felt a sharp poke in the middle of his back.

"Ahhh!" shouted Blaze. "The shark is trying to eat me!"

Blaze frantically kicked his flippers and swung his arms.

"No, silly!" said Ashley. "That's Daphne. She's trying to help!"

Daphne poked Blaze in the back again and squealed. Then she swam in front of him.

"Hurry!" shouted Ashley. "Grab onto Daphne's dorsal fin. The shark is almost here!"

Blaze reached out and grabbed ahold of the fin on Daphne's back. She squealed and flapped her tail, swimming quickly through the water.

"Daphne is pulling me!" said Blaze. "She must know of a hiding place."

"And just in time," shouted Ashley. "The shark is right behind you!"

Blaze looked over his shoulder and saw the wide-open mouth of the great white shark. The scar down its face and side seemed to flash red in anger.

"Ahhh!" shouted Blaze. "It has so many teeth!"

Daphne swam furiously over the top of the reef to the other side.

"The shark is gaining on you!" shouted Ashley. "You have to go faster!"

"Help!" shouted Blaze.

"I know what to do!" said Ashley.

She grabbed the lever on the control panel and pushed it all the way forward.

"Here I come!" said Ashley.

The submarine jumped forward and charged over the top of the reef.

"At full speed, the submarine is faster than you, Daphne, and the shark!" said Ashley.

"Hurry!" said Blaze.

"Just a few more seconds," said Ashley.

She drove the submarine right next to the shark and pounded the button for the submarine horn.

"BEEEEYYOOOOONG!!" the horn screamed.

The shark shook in surprise and snapped its jaws shut. It spun around and swam quickly away, clearly frightened.

"You saved me!" said Blaze. "The shark is swimming away."

"The horn scared it," said Ashley.

Daphne squealed and slowed her speed as she calmed down. But she kept swimming on course, so Ashley followed her in the submarine.

"What's that up ahead?" asked Ashley.

Blaze turned back to see a large dark object rushing toward them—or rather Daphne was rushing toward it.

"It's a sunken ship!" said Blaze.

"Daphne was taking you here to escape the shark!" said Ashley. "It must be a secret hiding place."

Daphne squealed in delight and carried Blaze through a crack in the side of the ship's hull.

HIDDEN TREASURE

9

Blaze blinked his eyes and stared all around. He was surrounded by old wooden barrels, boxes, and chests.

"This is a secret hiding place!" said Blaze. "There could be treasure in all these old boxes!"

Daphne squealed and swam in a circle around the room. Then she stopped and poked a large chest on the floor with her nose.

"I think Daphne wants me to open one of the chests," said Blaze.

"Be careful," said Ashley. "There's no telling what could be inside."

Blaze swam up to the chest and tried to open the lid.

"The lid is stuck," said Blaze. "There's some kind of metal lock on it."

"Wait. It couldn't be...could it?" asked Ashley.

"What couldn't be?" asked Blaze.

"The key! The key from the lunchbox. We have to try using it to open the chest!" said Ashley.

"Great idea!" said Blaze.

Blaze kicked his flippers and swam out of the sunken ship to the submarine.

Ashley opened the lunchbox, reached inside and grabbed the old key. As she lifted it, the key grew and grew until it was as large as the lunchbox itself.

"This is amazing!" said Ashley.

She ran to the diving hatch, opened it, and handed the key to Blaze.

Blaze kicked his flippers and swam back inside the sunken ship to the old chest.

"The key fits!" said Blaze.

Blaze turned the key and felt a snap in the lock. Then he gently lifted the lid.

"What in the world?" asked Blaze.

"What is it?" asked Ashley.

"The only thing inside the chest is a metal cylinder," said Blaze. "It looks kind of like a Thermos."

"Well, it must be important if it was locked in a chest like that," said Ashley.

"You're right," Blaze agreed.

Just then, the submarine shuddered, and a giant white creature swam in front of the submarine window.

"Ahhh!" screamed Ashley. "The shark is back!"

ESCAPE

Ashley pounded the button for the submarine horn.

"BEEEEYYOOOOONG!!" the horn screamed.

This time the shark did not react, and it kept swimming toward the sunken ship. Ashley pounded the horn again, "BEEEEYYOOOOONG!!"

"It's not working!" Ashley yelled. "The shark isn't scared anymore."

"We have to get out of here!" Blaze said.

Daphne squealed. Then she flicked her tail and swam through the crack in the side of the ship.

"Look!" said Ashley. "Daphne is distracting the shark."

Daphne swam a wide circle around the shark and made several sharp squeals. The shark began to chase her.

"Hurry, Blaze!" said Ashley. "Don't forget the metal cylinder!"

Blaze kicked his flippers as hard he could and made his way to the submarine's diving hatch. He grabbed the edge of the hatch and quickly pulled himself inside the submarine.

"Whew! That was close," said Blaze.

He closed the hatch door and then put the butterfly net, the key, the pink coral, and the metal cylinder next to the lunchbox.

"It's not over yet!" said Ashley.

Blaze ran to the submarine window just in time to see Daphne race past. The shark was close behind.

"Oh no!" said Blaze.

"Come on, Daphne. You can make it!" shouted Ashley.

Daphne swam furiously toward the sunken ship and dove through the crack in its side. The shark rammed into the side of the ship with a loud THUNK but couldn't fit through the hole. It swam angrily back and forth in front of the hole then swam away in frustration.

"Yay! Daphne is safe!" shouted Ashley.

"Daphne saved me!" said Blaze. Then he shouted, "Thank you!"

Daphne squealed in delight one last time.

HOMEWARD BOUND

11

"I think we have had enough adventure for one day," said Ashley. "Let's figure out how to get home."

"The lunchbox!" said Blaze. "It took us here. I bet it can take us home again!"

"You're right!" said Ashley. "But how do we get it to do the magic again?"

"When we were in the museum, I said I wondered what it would be like to go on an adventure under the sea," said Blaze. "And that's when the lunchbox started to vibrate and glow!"

"So, maybe we just ask," said Ashley. "Lunchbox, please help us go home."

Blaze and Ashley stared at the lunchbox waiting. Nothing happened.

"Hmm," said Blaze. "When we came here, the lunchbox

was full of tools. Maybe we need to put the tools away first!

"It's worth a try," said Ashley.

She picked up the butterfly net and lowered it into the lunchbox. The net shrank back to its original size and fit easily inside the lunchbox.

"It worked!" said Blaze. "Let's try the diving suit."

Ashley helped Blaze remove his helmet and clip it to the back of the diving suit. Then Blaze pulled one sleeve off and began pushing it into the lunchbox. As soon as the sleeve started to go in, the diving suit began to unwrap itself from Blaze's body and shrink into the lunchbox.

"Amazing!" said Ashley. "Let's try the key and field journal."

She pushed the key into the lunchbox the same way. All the tools fit neatly inside. Then she added the field journal on top.

"That's everything that was in the lunchbox when we started," said Blaze.

Still nothing happened.

"Let's ask it again now that the tools are inside," said Ashley. "Lunchbox, please take us home!"

Just as she spoke, the lid of the lunchbox snapped closed all on its own. The lunchbox started to vibrate.

"Something is happening!" said Blaze.

The emblem on the side of the lunchbox began to glow. The glow became brighter and brighter, and the lunchbox shook even more.

"It's doing it again!" said Blaze.

"Touch the emblem!" said Ashley.

Blaze reached down and touched the silver emblem. Immediately, the air around Blaze and Ashley swirled. Their eyes filled with all the colors of the rainbow.

For a brief moment, they felt weightless. Then...POP! A loud sound filled their ears.

Blaze and Ashley both fell to the floor.

CATCH UP

12

Blaze and Ashley looked around. Through the window of the submarine they could see the Undersea exhibit.

"We made it back!" said Blaze. "I can see the class and Miss Amy."

"And look at the clock!" pointed Ashley. "It still says 12:55! No time has passed since we left."

Blaze and Ashley looked at each other and then at the lunchbox in amazement.

"Do you think anyone will believe us if we tell them what happened?" Blaze asked.

"Probably not. But we know it happened," said Ashley.

Blaze opened the lunchbox.

"The tools are still here," he said.

Blaze reached into the lunchbox and pulled out the miniature diving suit.

"Huh?" said Blaze. "Nothing is happening. It's still tiny."

"It must be part of the magic," said Ashley. "We needed the tools for the adventure. But now the adventure is over."

"You're right," said Blaze. "But I better save the tools in case we need them again in the future."

Blaze clipped the miniature diving suit onto the shoulder strap of the lunchbox. Then he did the same with the net and key.

"Hey, look at this!" Ashley said as she picked up the metal cylinder. "The lid on this metal thing comes off."

"It *is* a Thermos!" said Blaze. "Just like I thought. Is there anything inside?"

Ashley unscrewed the lid, and a rolled-up piece of paper fell out of the open Thermos. It had a torn edge as if it had been ripped from a book.

"The Thermos must have protected the paper from the water this whole time," said Ashley.

"What does it say?" asked Blaze.

Ashley unrolled the paper to reveal a beautifully penned letter. It read:

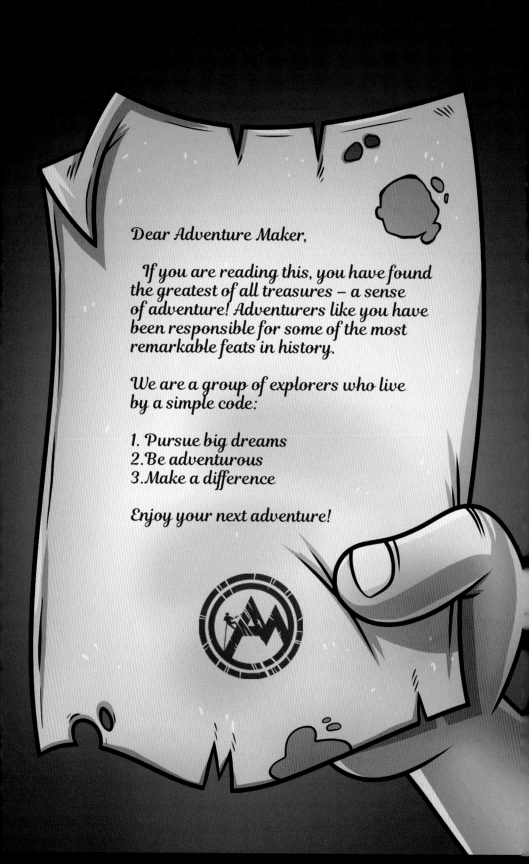

Dear Adventure Maker,

If you are reading this, you have found the greatest of all treasures – a sense of adventure! Adventurers like you have been responsible for some of the most remarkable feats in history.

We are a group of explorers who live by a simple code:

1. Pursue big dreams
2. Be adventurous
3. Make a difference

Enjoy your next adventure!

"Did you see the emblem at the bottom of the letter?" asked Ashley.

"It's the same as the silver emblem on the side of the lunchbox!" exclaimed Blaze.

"And look!" said Ashley, "The letter has a torn edge."

Ashley opened the lunchbox and pulled the field journal out. She flipped to the end of the journal. Then she lined up the jagged edge of the letter with the jagged edge of the torn page from the end of the journal.

"It fits perfectly!" she said. "The person who wrote the letter must be the same person who wrote the notes in the field journal!"

"Wait a minute," said Blaze. "We found hidden treasure in a secret sunken ship. That's just like the adventurer that Miss Amy described to the class. Could the letter be from the adventurer who mysteriously disappeared?"

Ashley and Blaze looked at each other in wonder.

DONG! The clock chimed 1:00 P.M.

"Class, gather around," said Miss Amy. "It's time to move on to the next exhibit."

"I can't wait to see the next exhibit," said Ashley.

"Maybe the lunchbox will take us on another adventure," said Blaze.

"Let's go!" they said together.

THE END

UNDERSEA FIELD JOURNAL

This field journal provides undersea facts and fun activities just like the journal Blaze and Ashley found in the lunchbox. Enjoy!

FIELD JOURNAL CONTENTS

1. Tools for Success

2. Submarine Operation

3. Ocean Encounters

4. Observations

5. Activities

TOOLS FOR SUCCESS

DEEP-SEA DIVING SUIT:

- Airtight suit worn by a diver in the ocean

- Oxygen tank allows the diver to breathe underwater

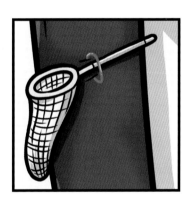

BUTTERFLY NET:

- Used to catch fish or other small creatures

SKELETON KEY:

- Opens locks

SUBMARINE OPERATION

CONTROL PANEL INSIDE SUBMARINE:

SUBMARINE CONTROL PANEL INCLUDES:

- Lever for propeller speed: push it to go forward, pull it for reverse.

- A steering wheel to turn the exterior fins that move the submarine left, right, up, and down.

- Intercom to allow communication with divers.

- Horn to warn of danger.

EXTERNAL VIEW OF SUBMARINE:

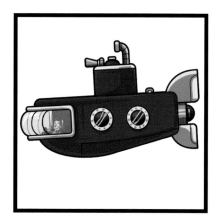

SUBMARINE:

- A submarine is a boat that operates underwater.

- A propeller on the back moves the submarine.

- Controllable fins help steer the boat.

- Viewing windows and portholes allow sailors to see outside.

- A hatch at the top allows sailors to enter the submarine at the surface.

- A diving hatch at the bottom allows divers to exit the submarine under water without letting air escape.

- Treasure hunters sometimes use submarines to find treasure in sunken ships.

OCEAN ENCOUNTERS

CORAL REEF:

- Coral are tiny marine animals that live in compact colonies.

- Their skeletons of calcium carbonate deposits make them resemble colorful rocks.

- A large group of coral forms a reef.

- Anemone and fish like to live in and around coral reefs as hiding places from predators.

ANEMONE:

- Animals with a trunk base found in coral reefs that resemble a plant.

- Their tentacles resemble hair.

- Can be many different colors including blue, pink, and orange.

- Can sting and eat small fish.

SEAHORSE:

- Small fish with a head and neck similar in appearance to a horse.

- Long tail that can grasp plants.

- The *male* seahorses (not the female seahorses) carry the eggs until they hatch.

CLOWN FISH:

- Bright orange fish with white stripes.

- Hide in anemone for protection from predators. Unlike predators, Clown fish are immune to the sting from anemone.

DOLPHIN:

- Large mammal that lives in the ocean.

- Breathes air through a blowhole on the top of its head. It breathes at the surface of the ocean and cannot breathe underwater.

- Swims in groups called a school or pod.

- Exhibits playful, social behavior.

GREAT WHITE SHARK:

- Large predator fish that eats smaller fish, seals, sea lions, and other marine mammals. Very rarely attacks humans.

- Can reach 20 feet long.

- Can have 50 teeth at any time. It has multiple rows of teeth in development, in case some fall out.

- Great sense of smell. It can catch the scent of prey from miles away.

OCTOPUS:

- Sea animal with soft body and eight long tentacles lined with suckers.

- Does not have bones and can squeeze its body into very small spaces.

- Changes color to blend with its surroundings.

- Shoots black ink to confuse predators and escape from danger.

- Highly intelligent and can solve puzzles.

OBSERVATIONS

New Undersea Creature: Imagine you are in a submarine on an undersea adventure and discover a new sea creature. What is it? Describe it here.

_____

_____

_____

_____

_____

Sunken Ship: Imagine you are exploring a sunken ship. What things might you discover?

_____

_____

_____

_____

_____

ACTIVITIES

WORD FIND: Look for the following key words from the story in the grid below:

ANEMONE   DOLPHIN   SHARK

CLOWN FISH   OCTOPUS   SUBMARINE

CORAL REEF   SEAHORSE   TREASURE

```
C O R A L R E E F Z R
C G U S E A H O R S E
L I E B J X T M D P F
O T O C T O P U S J L
W X M K S H A R K E G
N Q S U B M A R I N E
F A G O C Y D A Q Y Y
I D Z C D O L P H I N
S Z V J E W M Y C F P
H A T R E A S U R E R
D E K Y A N E M O N E
```

WORD CROSS: Fill in the undersea words from the clues below:

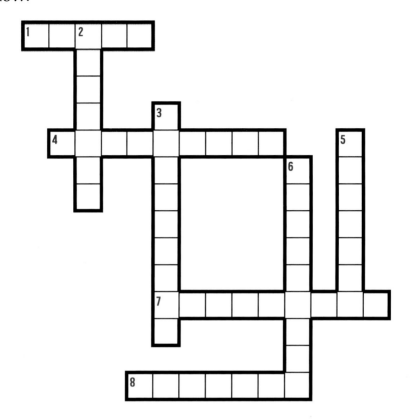

Across:

1. Has 50 sharp teeth at any time and more rows of teeth developing

4. Resembles colorful underwater rocks

7. Boat that operates under water

8. Has 8 long arms lined with suckers

Down:

2. Animal with a trunk-shaped body and colorful tentacles resembling hair

3. A fish that lives in anemone and is immune to its sting

5. Playful large mammal living in the sea

6. These types of boy fish carry eggs until they hatch

MAZE:

HELP BLAZE AND DAPHNE ESCAPE THE SHARK BY NAVIGATING THE CORAL REEF MAZE TO THE SUBMARINE!

START

END

PICTURE FIND: Help Blaze find all 10 octopus babies in the picture below.

ABOUT THE AUTHORS

Twins Adam and Andrew Peeples are excited to write the *Lunchbox Adventures* series together. Both live in Columbus, Ohio, and both are happy fathers of young children who bring them joy every day. Adam and Andrew hope that the *Lunchbox Adventures* will inspire their kids and others around the world to pursue big dreams, be adventurous, and make a difference.

ABOUT THE ILLUSTRATOR

Andrew Laitinen has been drawing since a young age. As an up-and-coming artist fresh out of the Columbus College of Art and Design Illustration Program, he strives to create artwork that is uplifting and brings joy to children and parents.

He currently resides in Albany, NY with his wife, Florence, and Freddy the goldendoodle.

LUNCHBOX *Adventures*®

2

FLY HIGH

WRITTEN BY: ADAM & ANDREW PEEPLES
ARTWORK BY: ANDREW LAITINEN

LUNCHBOX *Adventures*® 2

FLY HIGH

COMING SOON...

Famous British inventor Sir George Cayley is attempting to be the first to fly a fixed-wing aircraft. He needs help!

Join Blaze and Ashley as the magic lunchbox takes them on an adventure to an important moment in the history of flight over 150 years ago.

Will they crash? Or will they be the first to fly? Find out in *Fly High*!